nest

Jorey Hurley

A Paula Wiseman Book

Simon & Schuster Books for Young Readers

New York London Toronto Sydney New Delhi

nest

warm

hatch

grow

jump

fly

feast

surprise

blow

snuggle

sleep

awake

explore

meet

nest

for alder and holden

SIMON & SCHUSTER BOOKS FOR YOUNG READERS • An imprint of Simon & Schuster Children's Publishing Division • 1230 Avenue of the Americas, New York, New York 10020 • Copyright © 2014 by Jorey Hurley • All rights reserved, including the right of reproduction in whole or in part in any form. • SIMON & SCHUSTER BOOKS FOR YOUNG READERS is a trademark of Simon & Schuster, Inc. • For information about special discounts for bulk purchases, please contact Simon & Schuster Special Sales at 1-866-506-1949 or business@simonandschuster.com. • The Simon & Schuster Speakers Bureau can bring authors to your live event. For more information or to book an event, contact the Simon & Schuster Speakers Bureau at 1-866-248-3049 or visit our website at www.simonspeakers.com. • Book design by Lizzy Bromley • The text for this book is set in Goldenbook. • The illustrations for this book are rendered in Photoshop. • Manufactured in China • 1113 SCP • 10 9 8 7 6 5 4 3 2 1 • Library of Congress Cataloging-in-Publication Data • Hurley, Jorey. • Nest / Jorey Hurley ; illustrated by Jorey Hurley. — First edition. • pages cm • Summary: A simple depiction of a year in the life of a bird. • ISBN 978-1-4424-8971-4 (hardcover : alk. paper) — ISBN 978-1-4424-8972-1 (e-book) • 1. Birds—Juvenile literature. [1. Birds.] I. Title. • QL676.2.H875 2014 • 598—dc23 • 2012044005

author's note

This book started when my daughters and I began watching a family of robins outside our kitchen window in northern California. The American robin is common across North America and is found as far south as Mexico. It is easy to spot by its reddish breast feathers, which range in color from dark maroon to light orange, and which gave it its name. Early European settlers named the American robin because its red breast reminded them of the similarly colored but unrelated European robin familiar from back home.

Robins eat insects, fruits, and berries. The berries of the dogwood tree shown in this book are quickly gone, eaten by the birds. Robins are among the first birds to sing at dawn, and their song is simple and the sounds are repeated. Some robins migrate south during the winter to find warmer weather. Some, like the family in this story, stay in the same area all year, snuggling together to keep warm and eating winter berries. In either case, robins like to raise their own babies near where they were born, so any birds that migrated south for the winter return home by early spring to start families.

Female robins build nests from twigs, straw, and bits of paper and smear beakfuls of mud around the inside of the nest to hold it together. Once the nest is ready, she lays one blue egg each day for up to five days. Then she settles down to keep the eggs warm, which is called incubation. During incubation, she will carefully turn the eggs over every day to make sure that all sides are evenly warmed, and she will scare off any squirrels, blue jays, or other predators that try to steal the eggs. After fourteen days, the chicks hatch by pecking their way out of their shells with a special part of their beak called an egg tooth. The newborn robins are very hungry but can't find their own food, so both parents work hard bringing them worms, caterpillars, and other insects to eat.

After two weeks in the nest, baby robins are ready to hop out and start learning to fly. Predators like cats and hawks are very dangerous to baby robins. The baby robins' speckled feathers help camouflage them in the grass and their father stays nearby to protect them. Soon they will be flying well and finding their own food. By this age, young robins look much like their parents but still have scattered dark spots remaining on their breast feathers. They will stay near their family, although their parents are often busy raising another batch of chicks. During the day they look for food like earthworms by hopping around on the ground and turning their heads to one side to get better views (unlike humans, their eyes are on the sides of their heads). They also eat fruit and, especially in the winter, lots of berries. At night they gather together, or roost, in a group, or flock, and sleep in the trees. By fall their spotted breast feathers have filled in to be all red and they are ready to migrate south or settle in for the winter cold.

Jonas Hurley